Ark Adventures

oah and his wife think a flood
ht be coming, so they have built
g boat called the Ark. They are
g around the world to rescue the
nimals before it starts to rain.

's all go on an animal adventure!

For Churchdown Village Infant School,
Gloucestershire
S.G.

For Joe
A.P.

Reading Consultant: Prue Goodwin, Lecturer in literacy and children's books

ORCHARD BOOKS
338 Euston Road, London NW1 3BH
Orchard Books Australia
Level 17/207 Kent Street, Sydney, NSW 2000

First published in 2011
First paperback publication in 2012

ISBN 978 1 40830 561 4 (hardback)
ISBN 978 1 40830 569 0 (paperback)

A CIP catalogue record for this book is available from the British Library.

1 3 5 7 9 10 8 6 4 2 (hardback)
1 3 5 7 9 10 8 6 4 2 (paperback)

Printed in China

Orchard Books is a division of Hachette Children's Books,
an Hachette UK company.

Hungry
Bears!

Written by Sally Grindley

Illustrated by Alex Paterson

ORCHARD BOOKS

"Can you see the sign, Noah?" said Mrs Noah. "We've reached North America!"

Noah yawned. "I hope the animals will be easy to find," he said. "I'm feeling rather tired today."

"Poor Noah," said Mrs Noah. "Let's have a look in our *Big Book of Animals* and see which animals live here."

Noah opened the book and turned the pages. "Grizzly bears!" he cried. "It says they love honey . . . and fishing!"

He went below deck and came back
carrying a fishing rod. "Just what
I need!" he said. "A nice quiet day
fishing."

They sailed the Ark along a wide
river until they came to a waterfall.

"This is the perfect
place to catch
fish," said Noah.

"I'll sit on deck and watch
you," said Mrs Noah.

Noah lowered the
gangplank and
walked down to
the riverbank.

"Don't forget to look out for the
bears!" Mrs Noah called.

Noah walked along the riverbank until he came to a large rock. "This is a lovely spot," he said, settling down.

Just then he heard Mrs Noah
calling him.

"Look, Noah, bears!" she called.

Noah jumped to his feet. Two bears were wading into the water. They looked very strong and had glossy brown coats.

Noah watched as one of them
pounced – *SPLASH!* – and
held something up
in the air.

"He's caught a fish, Noah!" shouted
Mrs Noah. "That's the way to do it!"

"I can't let the bears beat me at fishing!" Noah muttered.

He untied his fishing rod and swung it in the air. The end of the line caught in a bush.

"Silly me," said Noah.

He untangled it and tried again.

This time the line caught

in a tree.

"I'm out of practice," said Noah.

He tried once more . . .

This time the line landed – *SPLASH!*

– in the water.

"Hooray!" cried Noah.

It wasn't long before Noah felt the line go tight.

"I think I've caught something!" he yelled.

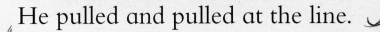

He pulled and pulled at the line.

It sprang out of the water. On the end
was an old boot.

"I don't want that for my tea!" called Mrs Noah.

"Oh dear," said Noah.

One of the bears pounced – *SPLASH!*
– and held another fish up in the air.

"Perhaps I should try fishing the bear
way," muttered Noah.

He waded into the river and peered through the water. The bears stopped to watch him.

"There's a fish," he cried. He tried to grab it, but the fish was too quick. "Missed!" he said.

Noah tried to grab another fish, but
it was too slippery. "Missed again!"
he grumbled.

The bears shook their heads.

Noah glared at them.

"Are you laughing at me?" he asked.

The bears grinned, pounced, and each caught a fish.

"It's easy for you," Noah said.
"You've got paws and claws!"

Just then, one of the
bears grabbed a fish
in his paw and tossed
it to Noah.

"He's giving you
one of his fish!"
cried Mrs Noah.

Noah leapt in the air and tried to catch it . . . but he missed and fell into the water!

The bears shook their heads again.

"I've had enough of this," moaned
Noah, climbing onto the bank.

"Never mind," called Mrs Noah.
"We've got something else the bears
might like." She waved a pot of honey
in the air. "Time for tea, I think!"

As soon as they smelt the honey,
the bears leapt out of the river.
They ran towards the Ark, grunting
with excitement.

"Save some for me!" cried
Noah. He grabbed his rod
and ran after them.

"Hungry bears like fish, but they like honey better," smiled Mrs Noah as they sat down to eat.

"I like honey better, too." said Noah, yawning. "Fishing is much too tiring."

SALLY GRINDLEY · ALEX PATERSON

Crazy Chameleons!	978 1 40830 562 1
Giant Giraffes!	978 1 40830 563 8
Too-slow Tortoises!	978 1 40830 564 5
Kung Fu Kangaroos!	978 1 40830 565 2
Playful Penguins!	978 1 40830 566 9
Pesky Sharks!	978 1 40830 567 6
Cheeky Chimpanzees!	978 1 40830 568 3
Hungry Bears!	978 1 40830 569 0

All priced at £4.99

Orchard Books are available from all good bookshops, or can be ordered from our website: www.orchardbooks.co.uk, or telephone 01235 827702, or fax 01235 827703.